JEASY ZELVER
Zelver, Patricia
Don Octavio and the new
creature

Withdrawn/ABCL

R'O GRANDE VALLEY
LIBRARY SYSTEM (W)

D0572676

JEASY ZELVER
Zelver, Patricia
Don Octavio and the new
creature

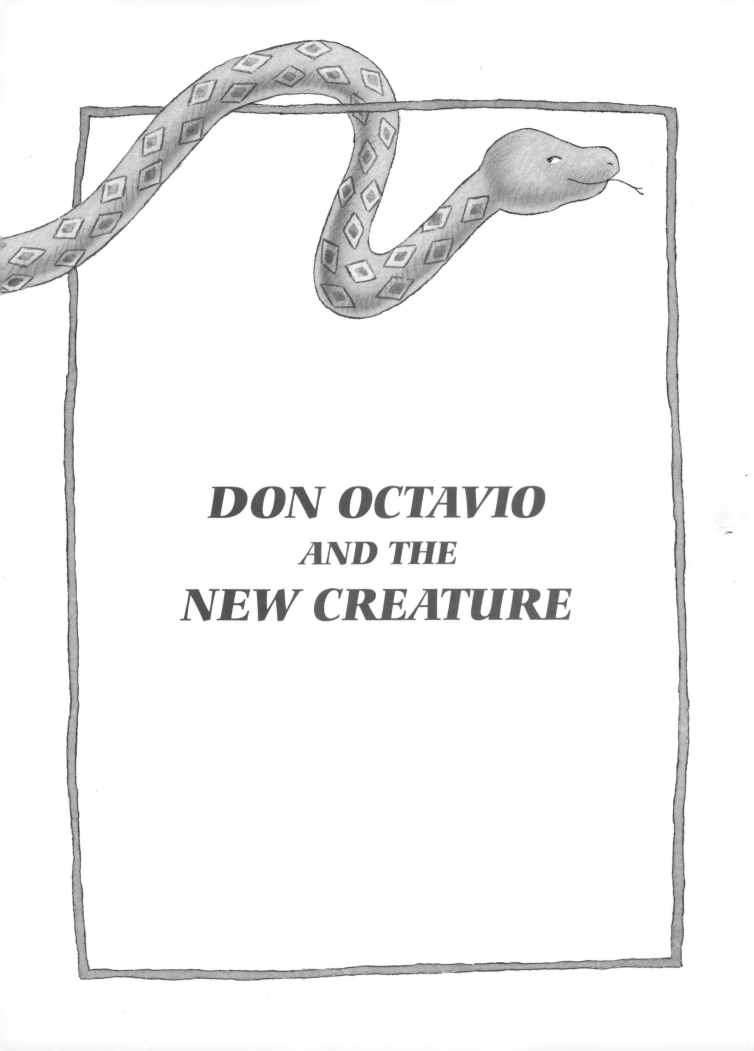

DON OCTAVIO
AND THE
NEW CREATURE

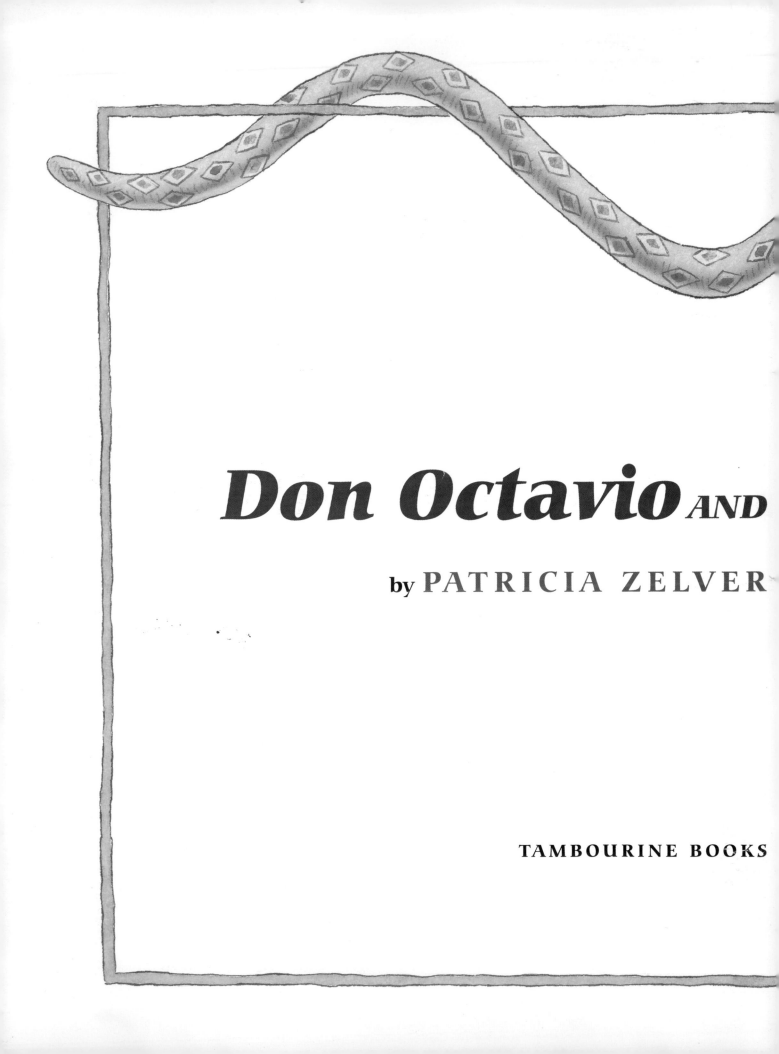

Don Octavio AND

by PATRICIA ZELVER

TAMBOURINE BOOKS

THE New Creature

pictures by LARRY DASTE

Withdrawn/ABCL

 **NEW YORK**

3 9075 01398 5889

RIO GRANDE VALLEY
LIBRARY SYSTEM

It was a hot afternoon in the small village on the edge of the jungle in the shadow of the great volcano. Don Octavio, poet and friend to animals, was making adobe bricks for the new room of his little yellow casa. Don Octavio's wife, Doña Clarita, the Lady of the Laughing Eyes, was asleep in the hammock on the patio.

The animals were taking their siesta too. Carlota, the green and orange parrot, was perched on a branch of the sapodilla tree. Paco, the spider monkey, hung from his tail from another branch. El Tigre, the striped cat, and Señor Gonzales, the yellow dog, were stretched out under the table. Violeta, the burro, slept standing up, and Don Sinuoso, the boa constrictor, was curled up under Doña Clarita's hammock.

Suddenly there was a great crash. The animals woke up. Don Octavio had dropped a load of bricks.

"What a racket," grumbled Carlota.

"It's impossible to get any sleep around here," El Tigre said.

"We don't need a new room anyway!" said Violeta. "One bedroom is enough for all of us."

Don Sinuoso coiled himself into a ball. "My friends," he said, "I do not think this new room is for us. I heard them talking last night. They kept saying, 'When it comes.' The new room is for a new creature."

"A new creature!" cried Paco.

"A whole new room?" said Señor Gonzales. "It must be for an elephant."

Doña Clarita was awake now too. She picked up her knitting and began to knit something small.

"She's making a new cover for my cage," said Carlota. "Mine is getting old."

"I think it's a pillow for me," said El Tigre. "Everyone knows blue and pink are my colors."

"I hope it's a hat for me," said Violeta.

"I could use a nice blanket," Señor Gonzales said.

"She's knitting me a little jacket," said Paco. "You can tell by the armholes."

"You're all wrong," Don Sinuoso said. "It's for a creature with four legs and it wouldn't fit any of us."

"I don't think that's very nice of them," cried Paco. "We don't need a new creature. Our family is just the right size."

There was a sudden howl from Don Octavio. He had dropped a brick on his toe.

"It used to be so peaceful here," said Violeta sadly.

The summer passed and the new room was finished. Don Octavio had retired to his salón to write a poem. Doña Clarita had knitted a little blanket, a pillowcase, two tiny hats, and another strange garment.

"It looks like it is for a rabbit," said Carlota.

"It certainly isn't for me anyhow," growled Señor Gonzales.

"All she cares about is this new creature," El Tigre said.

Another strange thing was happening too. Every day Doña Clarita's stomach was getting larger.

"She eats too many tamales," said El Tigre.

"I think she swallowed a watermelon seed," Paco said.

Late one night there was a strange commotion. Don Sinuoso, who slept at the end of Don Octavio and Doña Clarita's bed, was the first to wake up. To his surprise, Don Octavio and Doña Clarita were dressing and hurrying out of the room.

"Wake up! Something's going on," Don Sinuoso hissed. Violeta hurried to the window and saw Don Octavio and Doña Clarita getting into a taxi.

"Where are they going?" cried El Tigre.

"Why don't they take us?" growled Señor Gonzales.

"They didn't even say good-bye," sighed Paco.

The sun rose over the volcano, and it was morning.

"No one has brought me my breakfast," complained Señor Gonzales. "I want my bone."

"What about my bowl of milk?" said El Tigre.

The sun set, and it was evening. The animals felt lonely and cross.

"They didn't even say good-bye," said Carlota.

"They don't love us anymore," sobbed Paco.

Violeta sighed, and a big tear trickled down her nose. "There's only one thing to do," Don Sinuoso said. "Since we are no longer wanted, we must run away."

"Run away?" cried Carlota. "Where would we run?"

"Into the jungle," said Don Sinuoso.

"Into the jungle!" said Violeta. "How can we manage there?"

"Who would rub my stomach?" said Paco.

"Who will admire my beautiful feathers?" said Carlota.

"We have no choice," said Don Sinuoso. "We cannot stay where we are not wanted. You go first, Señor Gonzales."

"Carlota can go first," Señor Gonzales said.

"It was your idea, Don Sinuoso," said Carlota. "You lead and we'll follow."

"All this fuss has given me a headache," Don Sinuoso said.

While the animals were arguing, the taxi drove up to the casa, and Don Octavio and Doña Clarita got out. Don Octavio was carrying a little bundle.

"What's that?" said Carlota.

"I think they're bringing us a present," said Violeta.

"It's not a present for us," said Don Sinuoso. "I'm sorry to tell you, this bundle must be the new creature."

"They're taking it into the new room," Señor Gonzales said.

One by one the animals crept to the window of the room and peered in.

"They're putting it into a basket," said Carlota.

"What kind of animal is it?" said Violeta.

"It looks like a puppy dog," Señor Gonzales said.

"It sounds like a kitten," said El Tigre.

"It's kicking its legs and waving its arms. It must be a monkey," Paco said.

At that moment Don Octavio opened the patio door. He was smiling.

"Did you miss us?" he cried. "We missed you. Please forgive us, there wasn't time to say good-bye."

He gave a handful of seeds to Carlota, a banana to Paco, a bone to Señor Gonzales, and a bowl of warm milk to El Tigre. Violeta got her pail of oats, and Don Sinuoso, his raw egg.

The animals ate greedily. Don Octavio waited until they were finished.

"Now, I have a pleasant surprise for you," he said. "I am going to introduce you to the new member of our family."

He opened the door of the new room. "This way!" he cried.

The animals crept shyly into the room. Doña Clarita put the basket on the floor, and, one by one, they peeped into it. There in the basket, curled up in a little ball and sucking his thumb, was a human baby.

"His name is Alejandro," said Don Octavio proudly.

Doña Clarita picked up Alejandro and sat down in a chair and cuddled him in her arms. "You can touch him," she said to the animals. "He's going to be your friend."

"He'll love you, just as we do," said Don Octavio.

Carlota perched on the back of the chair and brushed Alejandro's head gently with her wing. Señor Gonzales put out his pink tongue and licked Alejandro's pink toes. El Tigre rubbed up against Alejandro's arms, and Violeta sniffed his ear. Little Paco took Alejandro's hand and squeezed it tenderly. Don Sinuoso crawled on Doña Clarita's lap and laid his head on Alejandro's warm stomach.

Alejandro made a gurgling noise.
"Isn't he beautiful?" Don Octavio said.

The next day there was a party on the patio in honor of the new creature. All the villagers came with gifts.

A man and a boy shot off fireworks. A photographer took a picture of Don Octavio, Doña Clarita, and Alejandro surrounded by the animals. Then Doña Clarita brought out a pink and blue cake, and Don Octavio recited his new poem, which he had written to celebrate Alejandro's birth.

"It's going to be all right," said Paco, sitting in Doña Clarita's lap.
"At least it's not an elephant," Don Sinuoso said.
Alejandro gurgled.